From Cubicles
2 Cabins

From Cubicles 2 Cabins

A survival Guide to your First Job

SANKET J DANTARA

SRISHTI PUBLISHERS & DISTRIBUTORS
N-16, C. R. Park
New Delhi 110 019
srishtipublishers@gmail.com

First published by Srishti Publishers & Distributors 2011

Printed and bound in India

Preface

This book is the outcome of one of those "Satsang" level (read philosophical) discussions I had with my dorm mates at 3 am as we spent the last few days at IIMA. We concluded that, 'Life is tough' and 'People are stupid'. And this applies to each and every one of us, no matter how smart; each of us makes stupid mistakes. And some of these mistakes are easily avoidable. There are thousands of graduates from various universities all over the country, who join the workplace with all the relevant technical skills. But is that enough? What else does it take to thrive in a competitive business environment? "And to find answers to this was born 'From Cubicle 2 Cabins, a survival guide to your first job"

What I have done is ask myself, colleagues at work and friends one simple question "What does it take to survive during your initial days at the workplace?" I then compiled all the answers, identified the critical elements and brought it to you with easy to remember phrases like 'Be the third monkey, 'Locate the spine' and 'Be friends with the gatekeeper'. Sometimes, we are blind even to the obvious until someone points it out and this is more or less what this book does. Show you the obvious. You knew these things somewhere deep inside you but didn't quite consciously and formally think about it. Well now that I have managed to keep your expectations low *(that's lesson No. 1 for you already, under promise and over deliver)* let me tell you why I wrote this book. Firstly, if you've never worked before, I hope to scare the hell out of you so that you join the workplace with more apprehension than you already have (which will help old timers like me to feast on you... just kidding!!) Secondly, I always wanted to write a book.

Any military mission starts of with reconnaissance, where you gather information based on which a strategy for the mission is planned. Then you go and implement the strategy, based on whatever information you had from your reconnaissance, which may or may not be complete. Sometimes you improvise on the spot based on the field situation. And then once you are done, you either cleanup (if you screwed up) or come back and brief the rest of the team to add to the knowledge repository that someone else can later use. This is kind of the way this book is structured too, though I leave the third part, the post-mission analysis (self – reflection) to you. I can't promise that you will conquer the workplace by reading this book, but it will definitely help ease the transition from being a newbie fresh graduate to someone who is comfortable in a competitive work environment. So enjoy reading it and if you like it, feel free to recommend it to your friends.

If you have suggestions, opinions and feedback on this book do feel free to email them to me at sankeyd@gmail.com

Acknowledgements

Thanks to my wife for her feedback, support &

Acknowledgement

Thanks to my wife for her feedback, support and having faith in me and pushing me to find a publisher. Thanks to my parents and younger brother for their support and help with reading the manuscripts and providing suggestions.

Also like to thank all my friends and collegues who read the manuscript and gave valuable suggestions. A big thank you to all who shared their experiences with me both on online and offline forums.

"As they say, leave the best for the last. A big thank you to **Mr Jayant Bose (Jayant Da) from Srishti** for agreeing to be my publisher and providing me with valuable guidance on the process. Not to forget the **team at Srishti** who worked on the typeset, cover etc."

Contents

Part-I The Beginning (Reconnaissance) 1

- Be the third monkey 7
- Locate the Spine 11

Part-II Moving Ahead 16

- The 3A Framework 22
- TASK 1 - Harness the power of informal networks 28
- Managing your own expectations 35
- TASK 2 - Gain visibility (2 down, 4 more to go) 40
- How and when to rock the boat 43
- TASK 3 - Recognize the power dynamics 45
- TASK 4 -Don't be so indispensable that you can't grow 48
- TASK 5 –Understanding your boss – what he says and what he means 52

- TASK 6 - Find yourself a good boss (swim through this and you can then dump the floats and head for the deep end of the pool) 55
- The secret sauce 57

Part-III Tying the loose ends 71

- Face time 74
- Communication 79

Part-I

The Beginning

(Reconnaissance)

"There is no excuse for incompetence"

I would have loved a job where I get paid loads of money for doing little if not nothing but alas *such jobs do not exist*. Even if I were to use alchemy to make gold out of nothing it wouldn't work, because the basis of alchemy is the Principle of Equivalent Trade.

Someone told me to add relevant pictures and graphics, so here is a picture of an Alchemist

It says "*you cannot gain something without*

sacrificing something of equal value". (Don't look at me like that, it's true. I picked it up from the Japanese animation series Full Metal Alchemist.)

Similarly, and sorry to disappoint you, there is no easy way out. So if you are lazy, incompetent, and good for nothing and are looking at this book to give you a short-cut or a sleazy way up the ladder (Trust me there are those but I don't recommend or subscribe to them) then this book will not help you in anyway.

Though what this book will do is give you a heads up on things besides competence and hard work that can make life easier. I will attempt to throw light on actions that can sabotage your career and how best to avoid them. (Ok, common pitfalls if you must call them that) At the end of the day, not all of it may be applicable or relevant to you and I sincerely hope you don't end up joining one of those organizations that have a bad work culture.

We have so often heard of this term called Organization Culture. So what is this culture that we keep talking about and why is it important? Organization culture can be loosely defined as '*the values, norms, activities, stories and so on that is shared among an organization's employees.*'[1] Once you join any organization, it is essential for you to understand what the organization is all about. At the end of the day an organization is made up of people; though legally it has a distinct identity, in reality, it is the collection of people that define the organization. In this respect, understanding of the culture will help a fresh recruit get the pulse of the organization. Each organization has a different culture and this makes it even more important for a newbie to understand the culture. If I were to summarize this book in one sentence it would go like this

> ***'Observe, understand and digest the culture, learn, adapt and then use this to help you grow'***

1 You may Google for a more precise definition.

Easier said than done, plus it sounds too abstract. Well that's why there is a book and not a quotation. So read on to know more.

Be the third monkey

"Eyes and ears open, mouth shut"

This should be your mantra for the first few days. Repeat it out loud and a hundred times if you wish but drill it in your head. (Incase you are wondering what does this have to do with monkeys, Google 'Gandhiji's 3 monkeys') When you join a new place, you will go through an induction, you will get to see vision and mission statements, value statements, process manuals and all sorts of documents that will help you do your job. But '*what you see is what you get*' might **not** always apply. Companies do sincerely try to inculcate a value based culture but it is not always so easy. There may be communication gaps, understanding lapses on your part. Many a times there will be grey areas. And most importantly we are humans and people have different motivations. Rationality is not necessarily our strongest point. (More on this later)

So look around, see what others are doing, even simple things like how do they dress, whether they use the cell phone in the cubicle or go out to a common area, if you smoke, where do others go for their whiff, how casual is casual Fridays and so on. Look at the work-habits, what goes and what

This picture ought to remind you of the mantra. Take a printout and stick it on your cubicle soft board.

doesn't, what are their attitudes, in short what the norms are. You may disagree to some norms, you may think you know how to do it better (you actually may, I'm not denying it) but this is not the time to bring it up. Later, maybe. So first wait and watch. Learn the way the organization functions; understand why the norms are in place. Nobody likes a new comer who tries to rock the boat on day one.

Your aim during this phase must be to observe the people and find out as much as you can about the work culture, the people, the nature of interaction between the various teams and so on. If you can find a colleague who will act as an informal mentor, even better. This is not that hard, usually when you join a team, your workmates will bring you up to date on the people and practices. However a word of caution, if you happen to be in one of those organizations where politics is rampant, you might get wrong and misleading information as well. So back to our mantra, eyes wide open. *'Listen to everyone but decide for yourself.'*

Locate the Spine

There are those who would contend that a corporate entity is a spineless, soul-less creature that would transmorph (if there is such a word) into any form to meet its profit making objectives. Still, locating a spine would be a good thing isn't it? Because this book is for conscientious, hardworking people. But I digress.

The spine plays two important functions in the human body, firstly it forms a vital part of the skeletal structure which gives humans the ability to stand upright and secondly it is the main communication expressway between the brain - the thinkers and the muscles -the doers.[2] Similarly in an organization there is a spine, the set of people

[2] For a detailed discussion on neurons and information flow via nerves and the role of the spine, the readers are referred to a biology book.

who give it structure, the set of people via whom the thinkers, the strategists, the higher-ups (read, the really big bosses) relay their plans and information to the implementers.

Now don't look shocked when I tell you that the hierarchy you see on the charts might not represent the spine, because that is what I was building up to and it should have been obvious by now. In a lot of organizations (note the use of the word 'lot of' instead of 'all') the power dynamics and the information flow don't adhere to the hierarchy charts. If yours is one of these organizations, it is important to know that this is the case. Because this one single piece of information can really play a very important part in helping you not only settle into but grow within the organization.

On a related note, an important set of people to identify are 'the gatekeepers'. I picked up this term from a book called 'Never Eat Alone' by Keith

Ferrazzi. (It is an amazing book, I highly recommend reading it) Gatekeepers are the people who guard the entrances of the gates you wish to walk through. Let me pick an example from Ferrazzi's book. He wanted to meet this very senior executive at a large firm. He knew that if he gets a chance to meet this executive, he could convince him and land a deal. When Keith first went to this executive's office, he started off on the wrong foot with his secretary. And from there on it was only downhill. No matter how hard he tried Keith was not able to get through to the executive. Somehow the executive was always busy, or in a meeting and so on. Later Keith realized his folly and set things right with the secretary. And soon enough, word about Keith Ferrazzi reached the ears of the executive. He gives other examples from his life as well.

The crux of the matter is, that *seemingly unimportant people can often give you the much needed leverage and at other times, rope to hang yourself with.* For those of you who watch the TV series Scrubs, you know how influential the janitor is! (For those of you who don't, I say have a life, watch it... kidding!) I am a person who naturally interacts with everyone without regard for their power status or job designation and so I don't find this astonishing. But if you are not one of those people who are naturally friendly with everyone, then the least you can do is treat everyone with respect. I am not for faking interest, being conceitful and friendly for selfish personal motives, that never does any one any good, besides people are not fools. However, if there is something genuine that you like about the person or his/her work, go ahead and say it. And even though this may sound clichéd *'Treat everyone the way you would expect them to treat you.'* I have followed this sincerely and it has only done me good. (You may also want to look at 'How to Win Friends and Influence People' by Dale Carnegie for other tips.

It's a classic and you can really learn a lot from this book)

Always keep in mind, that to succeed in any field, any organization and even in life, what matters equally if not more than your competence are your people skills.

So join work with an aim to genuinely make friends, friends for life who would stick around even when you change jobs.

So the mantra for the first few weeks is

"Study the organization and its people, make friends, and more importantly; avoid being controversial... tow the corporate line... go with the flow."

Part-II

Moving Ahead

Document VXI

"Hi, this is your mission commander. Here are the details for your next mission."

Mission Type: ***Solo***

Mission Rank: ***Z delta***

Mission objective: To survive the cubicle wars and put your career on a fast track.

Mission Brief : We already have gathered intelligence in the first part and initial reconnaissance results are back and look quite encouraging. Based on these results, to succeed in this mission, you will have to perform at least 6 known tasks correctly. This should give you a good starting point after which you are on your own. To perform these tasks you will have to master the 3A framework. Imagine a matrix with the verticals being the various tasks and the horizontals being the underlying skills required to implement them. The horizontals would be the 3A. The figure will give you a clearer understanding. To aid you further we have made available to you Document VXI with

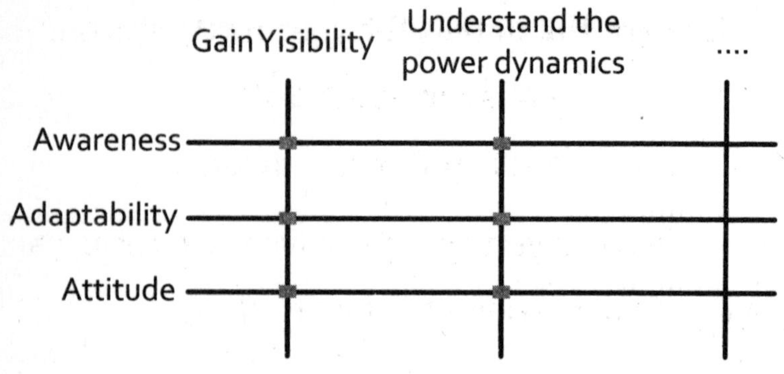

all the relevant information about the framework and the tasks. This information is highly classified and so treat it accordingly.

All the best!

Over and out

The 3A Framework

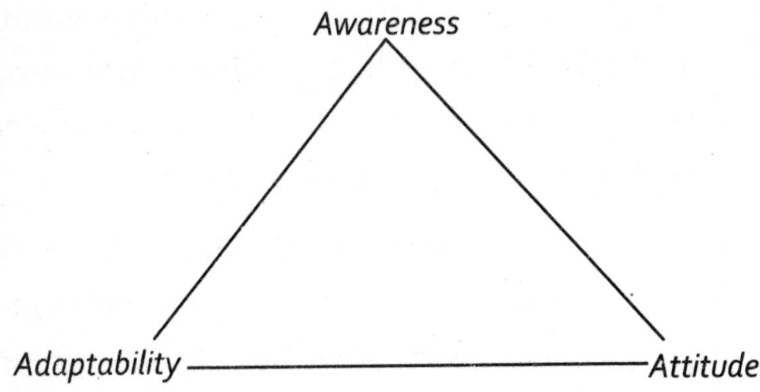

Have you seen a Tripod? Think of the 3A (Awareness, Adaptability and Attitude) as the legs of the tripod representing your career. Shorten a leg and the tripod wobbles, break a leg and it topples. That is how it is with your career. All three legs are required to give it stability.

Be aware of what is happening around you, both internal to the organization and external.

Know what is happening in the organization, what new teams are being formed, what new projects are being bid for, which project didn't deliver up to expectations, which department is doing well and so on. On the external front, know what is happening in the industry, where your firm is headed vis-à-vis competition, what new technologies are available and so on.

Why is this important? This is important because to move ahead, you don't have to wait for extraordinary opportunities but to seize the ones that come by and make them great. And unless you are on the lookout for opportunities you will miss them.

To drive home this point, let me give you a personal example from my initial working days.

I worked in a software company. If you have an idea about how software companies are organized, you know that there are projects and projects teams. I was in one such team. I started of as a team member and in a very short time I was a team leader. This transition was based on seizing many small opportunities keeping the 3A framework in mind. (Of course at that time I didn't call it the 3A framework. I formalized it when I sat down to write this book.) So, here is how it was planned.

'I kept track of what was happening in my project and so when the opportunity came, I asked my boss to let me train fresh recruits. This is notably different from and beyond my job description of programming. This adaptability to handle different tasks and the right attitude of going beyond my normal job as well as the task of training fresh recruits brought me in contact of other team leaders. These interactions got me noticed and when an opening came up I could go to human resources and asked to be transferred to another team where I knew there

was work which I liked.

If I had not kept my eyes and ears open, if I had not networked with the gatekeepers (referring to other members in my old team), I would never have known that my previous boss would be working on setting up another customer site leaving him pressed for time, giving me the opportunity to take up a larger role.

Not only internally within the project but this mantra of 3 A's works across the organization and industry too. If I didn't have the right industry and competitor information, at the right time, I would never have known that a new team (with work similar in nature to my current work) was being set up in another project. And most importantly, if I had not seized the previous small opportunities to inch towards a wider role, I would never have been able to leverage that experience to become a team leader for the new team.'

So you see the progression from team member to a team leader was not that of one big opportunity but that of capitalizing on a series of seemingly insignificant opportunities.

This one example hides within it a lot more information for you than just awareness. (Delve upon it; I'm sure you will figure it out. In any case I will point it out as we proceed.)

Though it would be logical to explain each of the 3A separately, if one wanted to operationalize the concept, it would be difficult to work with just these 3 qualities in isolation. Besides if I tell you be aware, be adaptable and have the right attitude, you will agree with me but wouldn't know what to do. So what I plan to do is, give operational, 'to do' kind of recommendations, (also known as tasks, we haven't forgotten our mission and its 6 tasks already, have we?) that require the 3A concept as an underlying theme.

Looking back at the example. Is it always possible to get such information before hand? How does one do it? (This is why we have missions, to train ourselves. So on with your first task)

TASK 1 - Harness the power of informal networks

If you have been paying attention to what I have been saying all this while, you should have realized by now

"Its collaboration and collaboration all the way"

You may step on others toes to make it to the top, you may employ the most sleazy tactics and make it to the top but then when you fall, there won't be anyone waiting down below to break your fall. Always remember, make friends. If you have understood this, you would have already found the key that unlocks the vault that has all the information you need. There is no faster way to get information than the informal grapevine. People love to talk, even more so when they have some important information which they shouldn't have known. Get the drift? (Bet it reminds you of those cold war spy novels)

When you do someone a favor, and they thank you, don't brush it aside with the usual "Oh, it's nothing" but instead let them know it was a favor. I can see the 'yeah right!!' on your face already, but relax. A nice way to do it would be to reply with an "Oh, I'm sure you would have done the same for me". (I picked this up from one of the old Harvard videos on communication, and it's a really interesting statement. Don't expect me to spoon feed you. Think about what this statement actually conveys. Hint: it ends with 'done the same for me')

You see, when someone has done you a favor, it is human nature to feel the compulsion to return the favor to your benefactor in whatever way you can. Recall of a time when someone did you a favor.

I am sure you remembered that at least for some time and you felt compelled to return the favor. Information exchange is no different. (In fact a lot of human behavior is transactional, based on a symbiotic 'give and take' phenomenon)

Well, if only life was always so easy!!! It would be if not for the petty office politics, which forms a cloak of deceit around the information you get. It will distort, modify, and sometimes render useless the information you get. So be very discerning with what you do with the information and how you use it. It is also necessary to differentiate between information exchange and petty gossip. I know it's a very difficult task, but keep in mind, bitching about others behind their backs, setting up others for a fall by spreading false information is not information exchange. In all interactions with people always keep this at the back of your head

"People behavior sometimes defies rationality"

Emotions play a strong role in the way people behave. Past interactions, personal likes and dislikes, prejudices, ego issues, and lots of other factors can affect human behavior in a manner in which you can't fully comprehend. I can't emphasis this point enough.

"Be very careful and discerning with the information you get and think very hard before you use it."

Continuing on the politics thread, there are these so called eternal turf wars between marketing and production or those between techies and HR. When things don't go as planned, the marketing blames the production department and the production department passes the buck to sales. If you are smart, you will try to stay as far away from these politics as possible. You may disagree, but I personally feel the best way to keep yourself safe from politics is to stay miles away from it. Don't engage in politics, don't support politics, don't take sides, just do your work the best way you can. Sometimes you may be dragged into it. (Tough luck, no book can help you there, you have to rely on your own instincts to make it out safe) Based on your individual temperament, you would have to find your own comfort zone. Know yourself better, find out your strengths and weakness, your competencies, your skills and then take a call on what you would like to do, how much you would like to engage people on such political matters. In either case, no matter on which end of the spectrum you lie, I repeat, make friends. On a similar vein, having friends in HR can be a huge asset. Think about it.

"Be aware, have information, but also know that office politics is a reality which can color the information you get"

Now go back to the example at the starting of this section, what other tips did I give you in that example?

If there is one single quality that can make the difference between you being able to successfully exploit an opportunity or fall flat on your face, then that would have to be adaptability. Adaptability with respect to the kind of work you do, the people you work with, the environment you work in, the pressure you are required to handle and so on. If you want to chart a steep growth curve, you have no choice but to keep adding to your skills and adapting to the dynamic workplace. You need the right attitude (willingness to learn for example. More about this later.) and the flexibility to stand tall in the dynamically changing environment. You would have heard this often, *'the only thing that doesn't change is change itself'*. Even without you wanting it, things keep changing, but here in this framework, you are actively seeking change, change in your role, change in your responsibility, change in the nature of work. And when you seek change, you need to adapt to the change to make sure that the change gives you the much needed chance to grow.

In order to do this, there are a few things you need to keep in mind.

Managing your own expectations

When you first start off with something new, have realistic expectations about what you wish to achieve. This is valid not only for all tasks we do but more so for your first job right out of college. Some would have been toppers in their batch, some not so. But once you join the workplace all that is set to change. By virtue of you being a topper, you can't ensure that you will still be the best of the breed in your team. You might find yourself falling short; you might find yourself no longer at the top of the food chain, (in a manner of speaking). To a lot of people this can be a huge ego blow.

Similarly if you haven't been a topper in college, doesn't mean you will not be able to do the task expected off you in the correct manner. Your college education was meant to do just one thing, provide you with the skills and it does just that. The workplace is the real test of what you do with them.

The first thing you will notice when you join the workplace is that there is a huge difference between theory and practice, between what you learnt in textbooks and how you use them in the market to make money. Depending on the nature of work, you may not use any of the material you learnt in college. You may have to start learning from scratch. You would be starting at the bottom rung, no matter how smart you are. You may even be unproductive for the first few months, or even worse, you may be on the bench[3]. Don't get

---

3 Bench refers to the time when you are in the organization but have no work. Usually used in the software industry to refer to the idle time between two projects.

flustered with this. Have patience. Look at this as a learning opportunity. It may take you a lot of time before you are handed the juicy work, the real meat.

What you need to know is that even if you have been the brightest of all students, from the point of view of your boss, you are still a novice. There is still lots you need to learn, and until he/she has confidence that you can do a good job, in all probability you would be under constant supervision and you would get only the bones, no meat. How fast you get to do the kind of work that you like is highly dependent on your willingness to learn. It helps if you think of your first job / task as a continuation of college where you would have to keep learning. Your grades would be determined by how well and accurately you did the task assigned to you.

Make sure you put in your best efforts even if the work assigned to you is not to your liking, is trivial, is menial, not fit for a person with a degree you have got from college. It takes time for your supervisor to trust your abilities. The quicker and more accurately you do the simpler tasks, the faster you will be able to give your supervisor a chance to trust your abilities.

It happens to all of us, more so to people who have expectations of very fast growth, we get disillusioned by the repeated trivial tasks so fast and either give up, become complacent or switch firms. This is the most taxing period of your first job. Have patience. Learn to motivate your self. Nothing beats self motivation. Any external motivation, is only temporary. So am I advocating that you silently keep doing the tasks assigned to you without a whimper? Not at all!

Free and frank communication has to be the foundation of your relationship with your supervisor. If you have a supervisor who believes in this, you are lucky and have a head start, but even if he/she doesn't, you can still be vocal about the nature of work that interests you. Subtlety though is the key. Convincing your supervisor of your capabilities comes next. So slow down, try not to learn everything in one day. Take it one step at a time.

"Have realistic expectations"

As I said, just knowing about an opportunity and having the skills to execute the task is not enough. Others should be aware of your capability to deliver.

TASK 2 - Gain visibility (2 down, 4 more to go)

Getting recognition for your work not only motivates you to work harder but also boosts your own self confidence and makes others aware of your capabilities. However, remember that at the workplace

"You are not entitled to anything"

You are not entitled to be praised if you did good work; you are not entitled to a promotion or a pay rise. The organization is not in the business of charity and entitlement. As often said, *'the business of business is business and only business.'*

So if you want something, you need to show how you contribute to the cause of business and that is why you need to make sure your work is visible. By visibility I don't mean exaggerating what you have done or claiming someone else's work as your own. That is plain cheap! But subtly make sure your superiors know of the good work that you have been doing. Know what gets noticed. At the same time don't let anyone else take credit for your work. There might be cases where you would do the groundwork and find something worthwhile, but your boss or some other senior team member takes credit for it. (This really happens, I know of friends who were on the receiving end) Remember, you can't win a fight with your boss; however you can take precautions and act smartly to ensure that your work gets noticed. You can make it difficult for others to take credit for your work. If you are smart, do good work and at the same time keep dropping subtle hints to the right people about your progress; it really makes it difficult for someone else to take credit for your work without making them look bad. (Worst case scenario, you can always blow your own trumpet, but use this only as a last resort in desperate times since such an act is usually taken in bad light and might cause others to think negatively of you.)

At the same time don't be selfish, if there was someone else who helped you, it is only fair that you share the credit with them as well. Don't be fame greedy.

While still on visibility, one sure shot way to gain visibility is to rock the boat. (I haven't forgotten, I told you in the first part, that if you want to rock the boat, I will let you do it, but at a later stage and now is that phase)

How and when to rock the boat

As a newbie you probably don't want to rock the boat, but if you have spent your initial days in the organization well, you are probably on a safe footing. You understand the workplace and you have now mustered enough brownie points to take a bit of risk. If you are sure of what you are doing, go ahead and do it, do things in a better, more efficient manner. Be on the lookout for problems that can be opportunities for you to showcase your talent. Be innovative, do things creatively. This is the fastest way to get noticed. However, visibility is a double edged sword, it can put you under a scanner, on the wrong side of some people and raise others expectations of you. So time it well, time it so that when it's done, when you have shaken up a few old practices, you are ready to take on the responsibility to see the change through.

TASK 3 - Recognize the power dynamics

It is essential to understand the power dynamics in any situation. Misreading this can land you in a troublesome position.

Take the example of Ravi Kumar. During his initial days, he used to share his desk with his boss. On one occasion the lead of another team was discussing some work with his superior. By virtue of sharing the desk with him Ravi was there. During the discussion his boss's stance was that something can't be done. Ravi had an idea about how it could be done and so spoke up, but to be immediately cut off with "speak when you are spoken to". The other lead was interested in the idea and so asked him to elaborate. Again being inexperienced he hadn't thought it through and that showed in his explanation. This time he was rebuffed with a "pura socho phir muh kholo". (think through before opening your mouth)

Ravi assumed that his personal rapport with his boss extended to the professional setting, which was not the case. It is important to define one's role in an organizational setting and understand the political dynamics of a given communication situation. With lots of observation and a little commonsense, it is not difficult to understand the power dynamics between individuals. Eat with as many people as possible, attend as many meetings with your boss and colleagues. This will help you understand the managers, their maneuvers, their motivations etc. However for those who are not comfortable with this intuitive approach, if you want something more formal I recommend reading

'Games people play' by Eric Berne. It's a very famous book that explains various social interactions using transaction analysis. (Sounds complicated, but it's very lucidly written and is not very difficult to understand)

TASK 4 - Don't be so indispensable that you can't grow

I started this book with one key premise, that you, my readers are conscientious, competent and hardworking people who just need some peripheral advice on survival. And I still stick by this assumption, so do all it takes to get the work done, be the person your boss looks to when he needs work to be done, however, 'don't be so indispensable that you can't grow'.

Now don't start getting so full of yourself already, everybody is dispensable in the long run! But any boss would like to hold on to a performer for as long as possible, because it makes his[4] task

[4] All references to he, him are to be interpreted as he/she and him/her. The masculine gender is used only for convenience sake.

easier. This is good for him and in many cases for you too, especially if the boss is understanding of your career growth needs and gives you increasing responsibilities. But this might not always be the case. Shiva M. was the star performer of his team in a leading IT firm. However he was unable to leave the team and move on to other projects even after 4 years on the same project (with little growth) because he was so irreplaceable to the team. It was in the interest of the company to keep him there. He finally quit. You don't want to be in such a situation especially if you like the company you are in.

"So do your best for the team but know when to hold back."

Some of you might say that this is unethical, unfair to your employer. I don't advocate not doing the work, because that is simply not fair. You are being paid your salary to do the work. What you can do is involve co-workers or juniors in the work, ensure that you are not the only one who can perform the task. Transition some portion of the task. You may be able to do it best but train others to be able to do it in your absence. Create your back-up once you have decided to focus on other tasks. Remember you have to make a tradeoff between personal growth and employer priorities especially if the employer doesn't realize your need for self growth. Besides if things continue like this and you stagnate, you are going to quit any way and that doesn't leave your employer any better off, does it? So take charge of your own growth. Move up the value chain in terms of the complexity of tasks, each time ensuring that there is someone else who will be able to handle the routine tasks. This way you can not only add value to your organization, focus on personal growth and also ensure that your growth needs are not in conflict with organization needs. Of course, if you are able to talk freely (without any negative repercussion to you for being forthright) to your employer about personal growth needs and they oblige, then that, I agree, would be the better alternative.

TASK 5 –Understanding your boss – what he says and what he means

The oft quoted *'Hear the unsaid, read the unwritten'* is so true in the work place as well. Not only with your colleagues but more so with your boss. Very often, the instructions you get might not be clear or maybe incomplete. Not because he/she wants to be mean to you but because they have made certain assumptions about what you know and what you understand. Very often a mismatch here can leave your boss feeling disappointed at your performance and you angry at not being told explicitly what was expected of you. This happens because each individual has a different work style and different strengths. Identify this and proactively take steps to ensure that you develop a work style that fits both of you.

Let me give you an example. Your boss comes up to you and tells you that he has a client meeting and is expecting a certain product ready for that meeting. Now what does he mean by ready? Does it include the user manual as well or just the product? Does he mean a demo of the product? Unless you both mean the same thing, this can be a disaster. For example you understood it to be a demo and he meant ready for delivery (which would mean the packaging and the user manual also have to be ready). So should you ask for clarification? Of course! Should you always do more than is expected? Why not, as long as it helps and doesn't make things worse. (Assuming you can still deliver on time) By proactively seeking to understand the strengths and work style of your boss and an awareness of your own style can ease the process. Managing the expectations of your boss can go a long way in making your career more fruitful. (You might want to read a Harvard publication, 'Managing your boss' by John J. Gabarro, John P. Kotter)

TASK 6 - Find yourself a good boss (swim through this and you can then dump the floats and head for the deep end of the pool)

Always know and keep in mind, that your immediate boss can be your greatest support system. He/she can not only protect you from backfires, but also catapult you to the big league, giving you visibility, helping you grow. So if you have a choice, find yourself a good boss. By good boss, I mean someone who has genuine interest in your progress, with whom you are able to learn and grow. More often than not, when you join a firm, you wouldn't have a choice with regards to your boss. However, if you keep your eyes open, it is not so difficult to find a boss who suits your personality and switch to his/her team. And this is where we again loop back and link to awareness. If not a boss, at least find yourself a mentor in the organization who will hand hold you in the initial days and guide you in tough times.

Reflect on these tasks. What is the one most important quality that you will require before even trying to attempt these? I re-iterate. Adaptability. In every sense of the word. You should have the flexibility to take on new and different kinds of work, you should be able to adapt easily and quickly to changing conditions, power equations and people.

'Evolution and growth stems from adaptability'

And so does your personal and career growth. Be as open minded as possible. Be flexible. Be open to change.

Adapt, evolve and grow.

The secret sauce

All of what I have said so far will come to naught unless you have the final ingredient, the third leg of the tripod, the right attitude.

"10 speakers can't beat 1 thinker, 10 thinkers can't beat 1 planner and even a 100 planners can't beat 1 performer."

So be the performer. Give it all you have, do your best, do all it takes to get the work done, have the go-getter attitude. You would have, I am sure heard a lot about having a professional attitude. There are however some traits which I feel are important. I have already touched upon these attitudinal traits in some form in the prior sections but I thought it would be a good idea to list them explicitly. These may come easily to some but they can be cultivated with some effort, no matter what your personality type.

Egolessness – Try to keep your ego under check. Very often than not, you end up making moves that are self-devastating with respect to your career, just because you have an out of control ego. Easier said than done I know, yet very important nevertheless. Having realistic expectations and not letting the first few months blow your ego out is very important. Similarly don't take feedback, too personally. If it is negative, don't hold your boss against it and get into a pissing match with him/her. Isolate the skills part from the personality / ego part and work on bridging the skill gap. Similarly, don't let the positive feedback get to your head and make you complacent. Remember, for every egoistic and overconfident hare, there will always be a hardworking tortoise!

Patience – Work towards your goal, sometimes the going may be tough, the fruits not easy to come by, but be patient, you will get your opportunity, keep your eyes open. Don't get flustered if you feel handicapped in the initial days, at times you will feel overwhelmed with the amount of information. There is so much you need to know, to learn, to come up to speed with the rest of the team. But remember, they have been there much longer than you have and they have been through the same thing, so be patient, don't try to learn everything in one go. Take it one step at a time. Similarly, don't lose focus if you don't get the juicy work at first. In all probability you won't. If you are a programmer, you won't get the design work, you will be asked to just blindly code, if you are a doctor, you won't necessarily get the complicated cases at first go, you will probably treating the coughs and colds, if you are an architect, you will not be designing the elevation on the first day of the job, in all probability you will be just filling in the lines and gaps. So be patient.

Enthusiasm - Be energetic, be motivated, do whatever work you are assigned to with passion. This is the only way to make sure you always put your best foot forward. Any slump in enthusiasm will undoubtedly reflect in the output you produce. Not up to the mark output, would mean you would still get the same menial, trivial work, which will lower your motivation even more and then it's a downward spiral which feeds on itself. A never ending loop until you do something to push yourself out of the rut.

Perseverance - You need to hang in there in spite of the difficulties, failures and opposing forces. Let's accept the fact, that life is tough. The competition is fierce, and everyone will try their best to come out on top. Sometimes it will be you who gets the gold, sometimes you won't even qualify. It's important to not give-up. Don't use a colleague as a benchmark. Benchmark your performance with your past performance. Do a skill gap analysis, figure out your weaknesses and strengths and keep chipping away at the marble bit by bit till you get the desired sculptured image of yourself. Everyone has flaws, no one is perfect, but that shouldn't stop you from trying. Keep at it.

Humility - Discover, analyze and internalize lessons from your past mistakes. No one is infallible. Of course you will feel elated when you come out at the top, of course you will feel invincible, someone who can do no wrong. But never let this get to your head. There will be times when you make mistakes. Accept it with humility. Don't get into a blame game. Take feedback from people you trust and have your best interests at heart. It may be your boss, your colleague or your best friend. Find out what went wrong and work on it. Learn from your mistakes.

Self-confidence - Have faith in your skills, competences and inner abilities. Be consistent and inspire others to emulate you. Never let external circumstances undermine your confidence. It is but natural that when you are new to the job, you will make mistakes. So learn from them. Ask for help. This is one thing that most of us don't realize. There is nothing wrong in asking for help. If you ask for help, you will find that more often than not people are willing to lend you a helping hand. Your senior colleagues, your boss, even your peers. Most people keep struggling and faltering and failing just because they don't ask for help. And why do they not ask for help? It's either out of over-confidence, or out of fear that other might think you are not up to the task at hand. And it is more often the latter. Have confidence in your abilities, and remember that asking for help doesn't in anyway undermine your capabilities, in fact it does just the opposite. It gives you a quick fix, life is too short to commit all the mistakes yourself, capitalize on the expertise and experience of others. It brings you up to speed faster, why then should asking others for help undermine your self-confidence in any way? Think about it.

Willingness to learn - Learning never stops, the day you stop learning, you stop growing.

If there was one tool that I was allowed to

pick out of the many I listed so far to take along with me, this would be it. No matter how smart you are, no matter how good your people skills, no matter how well you assess your skills and no matter how strong your self confidence and enthusiasm, if you don't have the willingness to learn, you will stagnate, vegetate and rot in the same place. When everything around you is in a state of flux, change is constant, when what you know is outdated in a matter of weeks, when your comfort zone becomes obsolete in a matter of months, when the very reason for the existence of your job profile becomes redundant in a matter of years, unless you have the willingness to learn, the will to pick up new skills, the desire to update yourself with the changing times, there is no saving you. What was once the fortress of human beings is being taken over by computers. I can find thousands of examples which will prove this point.

Unless you learn and pick up new skills there is no surviving the workplace. With thousands of fresh students graduating from colleges each year, with newer avenues for work, with the increasing globalization of the country, you can't afford to accept anything to be constant, nothing is safe from change, and neither are you. So keep learning.

Self-awareness - Know what you are good at and assess how best your skill can benefit the organization and your self growth. Keep in mind, the organization exists for a purpose and in the terms of goal priorities, the organizations goals will always be given higher importance than your personal goals. If you want to piggy ride on the growth of the organization, learn to align your goals with that of the organization. Assess your strengths and find out ways to leverage those strengths to further the goals of the organization.

Some goals may not be in sync, but if you spend enough time thinking about it, I'm sure you will figure out a way in which to leverage the organization's strength to further your goals as well. It is a symbiotic relation. Mutually beneficial. But for you to realize this, you need to know what is it that you want, what are your own goals, what is it that you want for yourself. Introspect, think deep and think hard, spend time getting clarity on this. I know it may sound preachy and useless, (I used to think so too, especially when people would go on and on about ephemeral things like these) but it helps. It's a part of your own evolution and growth, your step into maturity.

Open minded & looking for new things/ change - It is very easy to get comfortable & cozy in your job and do the regular work and then expect rewards for that average level of work. Sure, do those if you are happy with stagnation, but if you want to grow, actively seek change. Even if it means changing the organization, changing the job, changing the kind of work you do.

Ownership - Unless you have a sense of ownership about the work you do, it will never be your best work. This is something that you will find very hard at first. Taking responsibility for your own work. Back in college, it didn't matter so much. Not so now. I agree that this feeling of ownership of your work is also to some extent dependent on the work culture of the organization, but I personally have found that it is only when you have this kind of ownership feeling for the work, do you produce the best results. Ownership doesn't mean, not listening to guidance, not taking advice from others or getting things your way irrespective of the impact, but it means having the feeling that it is your responsibility to get this done right and in the best way possible, even if it means asking for help. If you wanted to paint / repair your house and you find that you don't have the necessary skills, won't you hire help? But once you hired the help will you just give them a free hand, don't you have a feeling of ownership? The feeling that, even though the actual work is done by someone else, the final output is a reflection on you rather than the person who painted the house in pink? It's the same for your work. Unless you get that feeling of responsibility, the feeling of ownership of your work, the feeling that the output produced is a reflection of you, it will be very difficult to produce work that will catapult you in to recognition.

And lastly,

Integrity - No matter what you do, unless you have integrity, all success will be short-lived. I know, what you read in the newspapers, see on TV is contrary to this, but unless you have your moral compass pointing north, you will never reach the top. Even if you do, it will only be temporary. We all know why the "Sarbanes Oxley[5]" act was put into place, why we have independent directors on boards, why corporate governance is the much talked about topic today, why even though a corporate is a separate legal entity, criminal proceedings can be initiated on its key office bearers?

"Ability will get you to the top but character is what will let you stay at the top. There is little difference between people but that difference makes a big difference. The little difference is attitude and the big difference is whether it's positive or negative"

5 If you don't know why, search for it on the net. No spoon feeding here.

Work on the 3A and the 6 tasks till you are comfortable implementing them. It will take effort and patience but the rewards will be worth it. A mission well accomplished

— End of Document VXI —

Part-III

Tying the loose ends

Till now, whatever we have discussed requires you to make deep rooted changes in your behavior, attitude and personality. In this part of the book, I will focus on the band-aids, the quick fixes, cosmetic changes that can be easily implemented. Here we will also try to fill in the gaps, topics that were kind of left untouched until now. Some of these will be relevant to each and every one of you, some to only a few. So let's start plugging the holes.

Face time

Some of you may already be familiar with this concept. Loosely it is *the amount of time you spend in office, just to show your superiors or client that you are there. It may or may not result in any actual work done during the time period.* Some organizations have people who still feel that the longer you are in office, the more you work and hence the more productive you are. The same applies to a lot of clients as well.

However a lot of organizations are moving towards flexi-timings, and output / deliverable oriented performance appraisals. In such organizations, it doesn't matter whether you are in office only for 7 hrs , whether you come in at 12pm or stay back till 3 am. All that matters to them is whether you deliver what you were expected to, in time, with the right quality. However there are still a lot of organizations that are not so flexible. Even if you don't have work, or have done your work before time, leaving early is frowned upon. It doesn't matter if you do only 6 hrs worth of work in the 12 hrs that you spend in office. If someone does 14 hrs worth of work in 10 hrs that he/she spends in office, you would still get a better appraisal because you were in office for 12 hrs compared to the measly 10 hrs that your colleague put in. If you come in to office on weekends, you are a hard worker. It doesn't matter that you had to come in on the weekends because you didn't do your work effectively during weekdays. Your presence is all that counts. It's sad, but true.

So, it is essential to find out what culture prevails at your workplace. What is the attitude of the person who is going to do your appraisal towards face time? As they say, '*When in Rome, do as the Romans do*'

Corporate functions Vs Departments

There is a set of people who believe that you are at an advantage if you are in the corporate functions of your company as against one of the departments, more so when your company is a conglomerate with multiple business lines. The rationale is that, since you are in the central / corporate functions, you would get access to information about the business much before the others do. Sometimes you would get information that others don't even get. Similar argument can be made in favor of being at the HQ as against one of the branch offices. Geographical proximity to the upper management is supposed to give you an edge in getting critical information which you can leverage to your advantage.

There might be some element of truth in this; however is it that important that you will leave the work you like doing to switch to another department just because it is located at HQ?? (Where you might incidentally get more visibility) or because it is part of corporate functions group and hence you have easier access to upper management? Well, it's a call you have to take. My personal opinion is that, on the visibility front, if you are doing good work, you will be noticed (have already given you a basic primer on gaining visibility). On the information front, if you have been making friends, information too should not be hard to come by. (I never even once mentioned that you need to make friends only in your own department / function only, did I?)

In short, in my opinion, being in HQ or being in corporate functions shouldn't be a primary factor in choosing the job. The role and nature of work should be the prime factor. If you have an option within your choice of work, then go ahead and choose being at the HQ over a branch office but never at the expense of leaving the work you like.

And this brings me to the last leg of this journey.

Communication

Official communication has been critical since the paper memo days. Now with the newer medium of emails (well not that new, but compared to paper memo?) and video conferences, it becomes essential to master the basic etiquettes of these new communication mediums. It would be beyond the scope of this book to give you an exhaustive list of do's and don't and generally accepted etiquettes so I would refer you to the whole lot of resources available online for these. However there are a few things that I would like to point out.

There is one very big difference between oral and written communication. A person if he/she so wishes, due to whatever reasons can always do a turn around and claim that he/she had or hadn't said / agreed to something. But when it comes to written communication, it is not so easy to repudiate. Does that mean that to protect yourself you should have everything in written form? We also know that it is not always possible to discuss, agree to every thing in written form. The acceptance of emails as admissible legal evidence has made it easier, yet it is not always possible. So here is what you can do.

Once the discussion is done and a verbal agreement has been finalized, send an email, detailing what was agreed upon to the other party asking them if we both have understood it correctly. The reply, if affirmative should be saved as proof, and if in the negative will help you clarify the difference in understanding if any. Of course, you won't do this for all day-to-day activities or for those that are within you purview of work but for critical issues.

You might also want to use this in another situation. There might be times when you would be asked to do things which if don't work according to plan might jeopardize the project / assignment itself. And then when things are going bad, you would invariably be the scapegoat even though this was not your decision and you might have done it differently. If such is the case, don't go ahead just on verbal instructions. Before going ahead, send a clarifying email which goes something like this

"as per your instructions, I am going ahead and doing blah blah ... however just wanted to know whether A or B should be done" or "just wanted some clarifications on your instructions to ...." Or something similar.

This way you can hedge your self against the downsides of decisions that might have been thrust upon you.

Make sure to save a copy of all your email correspondence, be it internal or external, i.e. with clients

Some more things to take care of before you hit the send button.

Are you sure the list of people who are there in the To, CC and BCC fields the people you want to send the mail to? Be careful when hitting the Reply All button. Sameer Shah, didn't check the list and blindly sent a reply using the reply all button, and ended up sending the reply meant to be internal for the team to the client as well. The consequences are obvious. You see, emails are a very tricky thing.

When you are having a discussion over email, with either one or more people and the length of the email grows too large, do you delete the older messages from the mail to shorten its length? Well you shouldn't. (I hope you know, for official communication, you should include the original mail in the reply and when each one does that the length keeps growing but it provides you with a full transcript of the discussion, who said what, at what time and so on.) If some new person is added to the conversation / discussion, the person who adds the newcomers should include a note in the email to the effect that he/she added X to the discussion. Imagine adding a person who you have been discussing until now to the discussion without informing the others. The newcomer would also be able to see the past messages. I don't have to tell you the consequences. Why someone would want to do that, you ask? Remember politics? Ulterior motives? Of course the other guy can always forward the discussion to this person.

And then there is the most interesting thing about email, the BCC field. Logically speaking I don't see any reason why one should ever use the BCC field in the office context. If the person is supposed to know about the content, mark him/her in CC, if he/she is not supposed to then there is no reason why they should be included in the discussion. Either ways the only time I can think of when one would use the BCC field is when you want to play dirty.

And finally. This goes without saying, check and recheck, read and reread your mail to ensure that the meaning conveyed is the meaning you wish to convey. Ambiguity if any (unless deliberate...well lets not get into the politics part again) should be cleared out. And the most obvious, yet we forget, spell check, don't use emoticons, check the tone of your email.

So what do we take away from this?

Be careful when using email. Make sure that your email conveys what you actually wish to be conveyed and that the right people are being emailed to.

Written communication, especially email can be a very important tool, weapon and shield in your armory to survive the workplace battle. So use it wisely.

With this I take your leave, hope this book was able to give you some useful tips and insights. Adios

"Work hard and work smart"